Five for silver
Six for gold
Seven for a secret
Never to be told.

THE MAGPIE SONG

LAURENCE ANHOLT
Illustrated by
DAN WILLIAMS

Houghton Mifflin Company
Boston 1996

Text copyright © 1995 by Laurence Anholt
Illustrations copyright © 1995 Dan Williams
First American edition 1996 published by Houghton Mifflin Company
First published in Great Britain by Methuen Children's Books,
an imprint of Reed Consumer Books Ltd.

For information about this and other Houghton Mifflin trade and reference books
and multimedia products, visit The Bookstore at Houghton Mifflin
on the World Wide Web at (http://www.hmco.com/trade/).

Produced by Mandarin
Printed and bound in Hong Kong

The text of this book is set in 19 point Perpetua
The illustrations are acrylic

10 9 8 7 6 5 4 3 2 1

Library of Congress Cataloging-in-Publication Data
Anholt, Laurence.

The Magpie Song/by Laurence Anholt ;
illustrated by Dan Williams. — 1st American ed.
p. cm.
Summary: Carla, who lives with her family in the city, shares a close relationship with her grandad
in the country through their correspondence.
ISBN 0-395-75280-9
(1. Grandfathers–Fiction. 2. Letters–Fiction. 3. City and town life–Fiction.)
I. Williams, Dan (David Andrew Neil), ill. II. Title.
PZ7.A58635Mag 1996
(E)–dc20
95–14792
CIP
AC

For my wife Jane
D.W.

For Alison, Nick and Sam – joy for a boy
L.A.

Dear Grandad,

It's noisy in the city. I can't sleep. When I look outside I see a million orange lights below.

I can hear police sirens, a dog barking, and the television from next door.

I thought about you far away in the country. Is it noisy there? Will you come and visit us someday? Will you write to me?

Good night,
Carla

Dear Carla,

Sometimes I can't sleep either. But it's the silence that keeps me awake.

I look out my window and see the black shapes of trees, and clouds racing past the moon. When my eyes become used to the dark, I see the whole sky is full of stars.

I think about you too, high up in your apartment. I'd like to visit you someday.

Send my love to everyone.

Grandad

Dear Grandad,

I don't like it much at school. I can't do anything right. Today Mom was late to pick me up and Mrs. Evans was mad.

It was really cold waiting for the bus. It began to snow, but it didn't make the ground all white–just muddy and gray.

At home the elevator wasn't working and we had to carry the shopping up all 574 steps to the apartment. When we got in, Dad had already gone to work.

Did it snow where you are? Are there any wild animals in the woods?

Love from,
Carla

Dear Carla,

Yes, it did snow here too. I'll tell you about it, but first let's talk about school. If the work you do at school is like the letters you write to me, then you must be smart. Your dad never liked school, but I taught him to carve wood and now he makes some wonderful things. Everyone can do something well. Just remember that.

The woods are like a magic place, as white as the pages of a book. They tell you the whole story of the night before, if you know how to read them. The words are animal footprints. I could see a fox had been hunting and some deer had been in the yard.

There's a family of magpies nesting in a hollow tree by the house. Do you know the song? "One for sorrow, two for joy . . ." There were three magpies this morning—"three for a girl," that's why I thought of you.

Write soon.

Love,

Grandad

Dear Grandad,

There are wild animals in the city too. Dad told me. He says when you work nights you see all kinds of things other people don't. Once he saw rats in the subway station. Some people sleep down there too, because they don't have anywhere else to go.

I asked Dad about the magpie song, but he said he didn't remember it. I've never seen a real magpie.

Dad says he will make me a bird feeder for the balcony.

Please come and see me soon.

Love from,
Carla

Dear Grandad,

Why haven't you written? It's your turn to write.

Carla

Dear Carla,

I'm sorry. I wasn't well. I'm better now. It was so cold here, I had to stay in bed. Then I forgot to eat. I slept for days. Guess what woke me up? A whole family of magpies were fighting by the hollow tree. There were so many, I could hardly count. Seven, I think—"seven for a secret." They collect all kinds of shiny things and hide them in the tree.

I'll tell you a secret, Carla. I've been hiding shiny things for a long time too. One day they'll be yours. Don't tell anyone.

I'm carving a little magpie for you. When it's finished, I'll send it.

I'm all right. Don't worry.

Grandad

Dear Grandad,

   I'm sorry you weren't well. We've got
a secret too! Mom's going to have a baby.
I'm glad, of course, but it means she
won't be able to work for a long time and
she's worried about the money. Dad
doesn't get much work now either.

   Yesterday Dad took me to see the
lights and look in the store windows.
They were full of wonderful things.

   Do you think the baby will be a boy?
I don't know where he will sleep. He
will have to share my room.

   I like your secret.

   Please remember to eat.

      Love from,
      Carla

Dear Carla,

Yes! I heard about the baby. I'm so pleased. It will be born this fall. I wish you could all come and live with me. There's plenty of room, but there's no work here for your dad.

I do want to visit you, Carla, but I'm still not quite strong enough.

I've finished the magpie and now I'll paint it, but not just black and white—magpies have a green and blue sheen when you look at them carefully.

I'll send it soon.

Grandad

Dear Grandad,

Thank you for the magpie. I love it.
I carry it everywhere with me.

Dad has been home all week. He seems
so sad. He says there are too many bills
to pay.

I asked him about when he was a boy
and he showed me a photo. He had long
black hair, didn't he? He said he used to
run through the woods like a wild animal.
Do you remember?

Today he's been making the bird feeder.
It's just like a miniature house. I can't
remember your house. Will you tell
me about it?

Love,

Carla

Dear Carla,

I'm writing this in bed because I haven't been very well again. Yes, your father had long black hair and he used to rush around as free as a magpie. My hair was once black too, but now it's silver. It's funny—I'm sure I saw five magpies this morning and the song says, "five for silver."

This is what the house is like. It's set into the side of the hill, so the back windows upstairs are just above the ground. At the front it's long and a little crooked. That's because it's very old. There's ivy growing up the walls, and the windows need painting. There are big oak trees all around, where those old magpies live. When I see them up there I think about you, on your balcony above the city.

I wish you could fly away to see me.
Love from,
Grandad

Grandad,

It's summertime now and you still haven't come. I hope you're not sick again. Have you been eating?

Mom and Dad are home all the time now. Yesterday a letter came. It said they might take the apartment away if we don't find some money. I hear Mom and Dad talking about it at night and I get scared for us and the new baby.

The birds have been coming to the feeder, but there isn't much food for them.

Please write soon.

Love,

Carla

Carla,

There were four magpies this morning, and I knew your brother was born.

The doctor won't let me write any more now.

Don't forget our secret.

I love you,

Grandad

Dear Grandad,

Why don't you write? You promised to come.

Carla

Dear Grandad,

Something happened. I woke up early because the baby was crying. I looked out onto the balcony and there was a bird there, a big bird. It looked like a magpie. He looked at me. He seemed hungry. Maybe he'd flown a long way. Maybe he'd forgotten to eat.

Then I remembered the magpie song –"One for sorrow." Grandad, I'm sad. You promised to come. Did you send the magpie instead?

Love,

Carla

Dear Grandad,

I don't know why I'm writing. It's been years since you died.

We love the house. Dad fixed the roof and painted the windows. He put the bird feeder in the back yard. He spends a lot of time doing wood carvings now. This morning I heard him singing the magpie song.

When I run in the woods with my brother, I sometimes feel you are here.

Carla

Dear Carla,

If you're reading this letter, you've found the secret! I knew you would. No one else would look in the magpie tree.

Show the box to your father. I carved six magpies on the lid. You know why.

Be happy,

Grandad

Dear Grandad,

There were two magpies on the bird feeder.

Thank you,

Carla

One for sorrow
Two for joy
Three for a girl
Four for a boy